UNREPENTANT TIMES

I0684216

Unrepentant Times

katakana
editores

Unrepentant Times
FIRST EDITION 2018

Cold © Alberto Chimal; *Euthanasia* © Erika Mergruen; *Rottweiler* © Isaí Moreno; *The Others* © Yuri Herrera; *Questions about the spread of mildew* © Úrsula Fuentesberain; *Kilimanjaro* © Lorea Canales

© *The proof of the pudding... is in the reading.* Elena Poniatowska Amor

TRANSLATIONS: *Cold, The Others, The proof of the pudding... is in the reading* © George Henson; *Euthanasia, Rottweiler* DR © Arthur Dixon; *Questions about the spread of mildew, Kilimanjaro* DR © Sivia Guzmán y José Armando García

© PUBLISHED BY katakana editores 2018

EDITOR: Omar Villasana
TRANSLATION COORDINATOR: George Henson
DESIGN: Elisa Orozco
PHOTOGRAPHS: Mike Vargas

ISBN: 978-1-732-11441-8

katakana editores

Weston FL 33331

✉ katakanaeditores@gmail.com

The proof of the pudding...
is in the reading

This book collects stories by six Mexican writers, the majority of whom were born between 1967 and 1972, the exception being Úrsula Fuentesberain who was born in 1982. Originality and the joy of writing abound in these stories, features that define each of these writers. Also present is violence, the thread that runs through each of these stories and serves as the watchword around which my friend Omar Villasana—the editor of this edition—has brought together each of these authors.

In "Cold," Alberto Chimal offers a lesson in characterization (the portrait of Cosme Valek is exquisite) for students of creative writing; the open ending and the humorous spark that runs through this story from beginning to end are proof of Alberto Chimal's literary talent, which has existed from the moment he was awarded, at the young age of seventeen, the "Becarios" prize by the Toluca Center for Writers. He has been writing ever since. Although he majored in Computer Engineering, and graduated with honors, he always knew he would be a writer. I met Alberto briefly through my friend Magda Solís, an amazing professor of literature who conducted a workshop in the home of Alicia Trueba, where Hugo Hiriart,

Rosa Beltrán, Juan Villoro, Agustín Ramos, Raúl Ortiz y Ortiz, Tatiana Espinasa, Estela Inda, and many others of today's established writers were teachers, who, in turn, have helped to establish students as distinguished as Rosa Nissan and Silvia Molina.

In "Cold," Chimal laughs at the charlatanism that is so prevalent and entrenched in a part of society that turns to unscrupulous characters like Cosme Valek in search of solutions to problems that range from gastric reflux to "love-sickness." The violence they exercise against whomever knocks on their door may not be direct, as can be seen in other stories collected here, and is perhaps less bloody but it is no less criminal: the good-faith scam. Chimal achieves a story replete with humor and at times sarcasm: "The thing is Cosme, by jumping from contact to contact, is finally making it big. He even knows some friends of Miguel Ángel—that's what he calls him, just like that, as if we didn't know that it's Miguel Ángel the big muckety-muck secretary, the most powerful man in Mexico—and any day now he'll be taking care of him. And later (of course) he'll still have Enrique." Added to the text's relaxed tone is an ending that leaves both the narrator and the reader "cold." Alberto Chimal is one of our most prolific contemporary writers. To his fiction, or rather micro-fiction, we must add his activity as an academic and his many workshops attended with feverish enthusiasm by young writers. It is not at all uncommon to see girls on the subway with their noses stuck in books like *Gente del mundo* or

Grey. He modestly states that he is a writer with "a few readers," but thousands of young people respectfully disagree.

In "Euthanasia," Erika Mergruen condenses a very difficult subject in very polished writing. The repetition of paragraphs to emphasize the comatose state of three characters is an astute literary choice, whose effect forces the reader to confront the same situation with different patients: a child, an elderly woman, and a man. The author rightly plays with the numbering of the rooms (the same numbers in different positions: 657, 576, 756), which suggests that her characters have something in common outside their vegetative state, a task that falls to the reader to figure out. Erika Mergruen—who is also a fan of microfiction—has published more than a dozen books and is a contributor to *La Jornada Aguascalientes*. In "Euthanasia" she manages to abridge a violence that we too seldom talk about: that caused by the death of our loved ones.

Isaí Moreno—who was a professor of mathematics before turning to literature—combines in "Rottweiler" the square roots of verbs and grammatical equations to deliver a story in which the reader ends up falling in love with Octavito, the tiny protagonist who is deaf in one ear and the owner of "Chiquis," the dog who sets in motion the tragedy that is foretold in the very first lines. Moreno introduces the topic of violence without reducing it to a morbid curiosity; even the denouement is proof of how one can discuss it without resorting to the grisly. Violence is present in the most unexpected places. How many Octa-vitos do we see in the parks and plazas of our country? What have we done to save them? Isaí Moreno, winner of the Juan Rulfo Prize for First Novel (1999) and professor at the Autonomous University of Mexico City, achieves an excellent tale with a seemingly trivial story: the adventures of two children in a park in the Romero Rubio neighborhood of Mexico City.

"The Others" by Yuri Herrera is proof of the NEW good writing that this author practices, which is confirmed in every one of his lines, painstakingly constructed and worked noun by noun. Yuri lives up to the saying that "literature is ten percent inspiration and ninety percent perspiration," and I imagine him sweating in front of his computer, until he decides the exact place to type the key phrase of his story: "She was my first girlfriend. The first I had sex with at least." From that moment the reader becomes witness to a tragicomedy, at whose denouement, just like the protagonists, he does not know whether to laugh or cry. Yuri Herrera, a PhD in Literature from the University of California Berkeley, is without a doubt one of the most important writers of 21st-century Mexico, and here as proof he provides a small sample of his immense capacity for creation. I know of what I speak, having seen him passionately a work in Alicia Trueba's workshop.

In her short story, "Questionas about the spread of mildew," Ursula Fuentesberain pays tribute to one of the many tragedies we Mexicans have suffered: the fire at the ABC

Nursery in Hermosillo, Sonora, in June 2009. The narrator
—a mother— focuses her violence in a long monologue in
which it becomes clear that the children were not the only
victims of the official negligence that still remains unpros-
ecuted, but also the parents for whom there has been no
justice even after 19 civil servants were implicated. The
creation of the female voice by which we come to know the
father and the dead son is an appropriate way of "opening"
the old wounds that this tragedy left on the families affect-
ed. Fuentesberain has managed to step into the shoes of
these women who feel, after the terrible death of their children, life is meaningless; without descending into melo-
drama, the author achieves a tense text supported by a nar-
rative voice that at times breaks and breaks the reader's
heart. At just thirty-four, Ursula has published an excellent
collection of stories, "Esa membrana finísima" [That very
thin membrane] (2014), with other stories appearing in nine
anthologies.

Finally we read Lorea Canales, author of the novels *Becoming Marta*—one of the best of 2011 according to the newspaper "Reforma"—and *Los perros*. Her story "Kilimanjaro" is
a game of feelings and betrayals by the violence that cruci-
fies our country and the double standards of Mexican society. Its title refers to the mountain of the same name locat-
ed in Tanzania (Central Africa) and formed by three volca-
noes, which hints at the trio of characters (or trios) that appear in the text: Luis-Margarita-Miguel, Miguel-Lucia-Mar-
garita. Without abandoning eroticism, she introduces de-

tails that suggests that the protagonist is fleeing Mexico out of fear. From whom and why he is escaping is the least important element of this story because the anecdote that Lorea ultimately narrates is a personal one that involves passions and anguish and that is—in the end—valuable because in it we recognize ourselves. Lorea Canales skillfully outlines the features of a woman from the upper-class in a key moment of her life and creates a flashback through which we are able to enter a world that, if at first glance seemed alien to us, ultimately we accept as our own. This lawyer and writer living in New York has had a brilliant career but has not lost sight of the troubles of her native Mexico, as evidenced by her work.

There is much truth in the saying, "the proof of the pudding is in the eating" or, in this case, reading: the six stories collected here are proof of Mexico's literary potential, and at the same time an incentive for young writers who will, no doubt, discover the rigor hidden behind every line. Many of these writers have a blog, like Ursula Fuentesberain, Erika Megruen; others write "Twitter-literature," like Alberto, who pioneered the idea of writing micro-stories and even micro-novels with 140 characters. All of them move about the web like fish in water; they are a generation of authors whom I envy because they have been smart enough to integrate themselves into the world that surrounds us.

This anthology will also be published as an e-book, a term to which I am still not accustomed but one that fills me with joy, knowing that it will circulate from web to web and that thousands of Internet users will be able to enjoy beyond the confines of physical borders, something so necessary in modern times when there are those who strive to build walls and close doors.

Elena Poniatowska Amor

ALBERTO CHIMAL

Cosme Valek is a pseudonym. A *nom de guerre*. A secret identity. Who knows what his name really is. I'm sitting in his office with white walls and a white floor. The table is white; the chairs, white. The calendar is practically white: the photo of the month is a white kitten; the numbers of the days are light grey. Next month's is probably a snow-covered mountain or a glass of milk.

Cosme is huge. He's wearing a large white shirt that looks like a tent. He's also wearing white harem pants and white slippers. Because of his big ears, I'd say he looks like Buddha, that is if his head were totally shaved. A black braid grows out of the back of his neck, long and thin like a genie from a lamp. That's his image.

The braid is shiny as if it were oiled and perhaps it is. The rest of his head is also shiny. Little drops gather in the folds of his neck. I wonder if he oils the rest of his body too. His belly.

I also wonder how he got his start. The thing about having gone to Tibet to study with the Dalai Lama is a total lie.

In his youth, Cosme might have been a student at some technical college or an employee of the grocery store chain Soriana. They probably called him Fat Man or Bear (or maybe even Buddha) and one day he simply had a revelation that changed his life completely.

"I told you before, 'alternative medicine' is bullshit," he scolds me. "Nothing but a scam for idiots."

He never talks to his clients this way, of course. He talks to them smooth; he convinces them with new age words, with the exactness of his diagnoses, and with the conviction he projects. He stands beside them, talks to them about health and about balance, instead of coming down on them hard and twisting their arm, and they feel better, even before they're cured of whatever ails them. They might have also called him the Refrigerator. He might have also been a snitch or even a hitman. Or a policeman. Perhaps one day he was burning bodies and suddenly saw the light.

"When you're sick, come see me," Cosme tells me. "Dude. Come here. Immediately. Don't go to anyone else. Especially since I don't even charge you bastards!"

The truth is he'd already told me that he wasn't going to charge us. And he doesn't: his secretary, the guy who does his accounting, his chauffeur who takes him to his big clients, they'd all told me already about their free consultations with Cosme. The thing is I never gave it a second thought. I supply him with homeopathic pills, so I usually skip him and prescribe myself (because I also studied a couple of semesters at Polytech) and now I wanted to give it a try. I thought I just had acid reflux, from drinking too much beer and too much stress.

"How many months have you had to sleep sitting up?" Cosme asks me.

"Four."

"I won't tell you how stupid you were. I mean, you guys are my family!"

I look at him from the chair where I'm sitting as my stomach burns from the inside out. He's really a fucking beast. I'm also happy that he doesn't hit me while he talks to me about fraternity and solidarity. I'm one of the ones who's worked with him the longest. Before this office he (supposedly) had another one at Merced market and that's where he started to make it big, but that first phase didn't last long. A year or two. They say. There are people who never go beyond passing out love potions or supposedly curing Aids in some disgusting little stand among the butcher shops and some market trash dumpster.

The thing is Cosme is "different": he has a special and unique quality. Everyone tells us we're special, of course, that we're all "different," but if that were true those of us who are mediocre wouldn't exist. When he says it it's true.

What's different isn't just that Cosme is always right and all his patients get better. Every curandero and healer and the like are infallible because people want to believe and they tell them they're right even when they aren't. That's what happened to my Uncle Toño: a witch had "cured" his cancer and two months later, as he was dying from cancer, he swore and swore that it must have been another cancer, not the one the witch cured him of.

No: Cosme is different in the way he examines his patients.

"Did you bring the clothes?" he asks me. For a moment I don't understand him and I make a face. "Sweaty clothes, dude."

"Oh, yes!" Before coming I went to my mom's house to use her treadmill. She uses it as a clothesline. Our family isn't big on exercise. But I was able to determine that it still works. After thirty minutes my heart was beating like a machine gun, my legs wouldn't hold me up, and my "exercise" clothes (in fact they're old pajamas) were soaking wet. My mother offered to wash them. She also asked if I was going to come see her more often. Even if it was just to use the machine.

"No and no," I answered. I had a hard time getting the pajamas away from her. I also had a hard time leaving.

Now I take out the bag from Comercial Mexicana that I brought the clothes in. I give them to Cosme. I'm still seated and I'm still intimidated by how big he is. Giving him the bag is like making an offering in a temple. I could say that I'm like an Aztec priest. Except we're in this white office in Colonia Condesa, I'm dressed like a Mexican and Cosme like a genie from a lamp.

Cosme goes to take the clothes out of the bag. He pauses. He then changes his mind, sticks his head in the bag and takes a deep breath. When he looks up again he has a

strange look on his face, which all esoterists should have
so their patients will believe them. But his is real. He's not
under his own control. One of his eyes moves to the left.
The other one continues to look ahead and the pupil di-
lates. He says he doesn't know how to describe it, but only
in private. He tells his clients that it's how he makes contact with the forces of the Universe.

Cosme recognizes people's diseases by smelling their
sweat.

"It has a scientific basis," he always tell us. He tells his
clients the same. It seems to be true. What we carry in our
body determines how our sweat stinks.

I look at him from below. He doesn't look at me. I wonder if he has tits, like other fat guys. I also wonder if he
oils them.

And I wonder, of course, what he's going to tell me. The
guy who does the accounting says that Cosme not only
detects illnesses. He can also see the past. And the future.
But the guy who does the accounting is a bit off in the head:
he wears earrings with feathers and in his free time goes
to the Ajusco volcano to hug trees.

Cosme's face grows blank. His eyes close halfway. His
lips quiver. His double chin also quivers. It's oiled (perhaps)
and covered with tiny hairs. Or he didn't shave this morning and they grow really fast.

Now he opens his eyes. He looks at me. His nostrils
flare out.

I remember that I didn't shower at my mother's house. Cosme bends toward me and buries his nose in my armpit.

I immediately tense up. I think I'm shaking a little. This intimate contact isn't that strange. Sometimes he needs to be sure of the diagnosis, he says. He has to do it with one out of ten or twelve of his patients. It's like gathering more data, he says, from close up. The secretary told me that he had to do it with a hot shot client. She didn't say who but it must have been a real hot shot.

"The bodyguards go real crazy when that happens," he told me. I wonder if the client was Rafael, the undersecretary. Or Carmelo, the vice admiral. Or the son of some millionaire or a society lady. Those are the worse.

The thing is Cosme, by jumping from contact to contact, is finally making it big. He even knows some friends of Miguel Ángel—that's what he calls him, just like that, as if we didn't know that it's Miguel Ángel the big muckety-muck secretary, the most powerful man in Mexico— and any day now he'll be taking care of him. And later (of course) he'll still have Enrique. Then he'll move to even bigger and whiter office in a nicer neighborhood.And he'll get rid of all of us who are his friends in order to get better ones.

These bitter thoughts run through my head because Cosme won't take his face out of my armpit.

He takes it out.

He places it between my legs.

I feel him breath in the air. I close my eyes. I begin to think of something else the accountant told me. That there are people with powers among us. A few. Sad cases. One day they receive a revelation and God blesses them. Gives them power. Sends them out to use that power for good. They don't have an option. But... Sad case. God blesses them and sends them out, but they have to hide. They can't reveal their blessing. They have to pretend they're scam artists while they do good. Sad, sad cases. If they revealed all their power, the others—the false prophets, the quacks, the politicians—would hate them and do anything possible to destroy them.

Sad case.

"Oh," Cosme says, after removing his face from my crotch. "Sometimes this is really humiliating." And then: "I hope it didn't bother you too much."

I relax in the chair. A little.

He tells me that yes, it is after all reflux, but a really nasty reflux. I have to take Almax and go to the doctor.

(That's also part of how Cosme's "different." He's probably the only healer in the world who from time to time sends his patients to the doctor. When a doctor is the best option. He says.)

"I can see things," he says, "besides what's wrong with your stomach. Damn obstruction."

"What?"

"I can see part of your past, who you are and your future." I notice his eye is still off to the side and dilated. "Can

I tell you more? Do you want me to?"

I'm unable to relax. This is humiliating.

"Like what?" I ask.

"I know when you're going to die. It's not soon. Not to-day or tomorrow. Or the next. It'll be years. But it will hap-pen. Of course. Do you want me to tell you?"

"No!"

Cosme blinks. His eye is returning to normal.

"People always say the same," he complains. "No one wants to know." He blinks again. "But there is something I must tell you."

I'm finally about to relax. I fold my arms and rest them on the chair.

"Let's see, how I can say this… One: your mother has al-ways known and doesn't care. Two: the truth is it's very flattering, but… no, dude. I like women. And you wouldn't be my type. I might as well tell you. I like 'em fat."

I begin to feel cold. Really. Really. Cold. I'm in the moun-tains from the calendar. The ones I've yet to see. I remember a lot of moments. I think about his back. Wide and white. Is his back oiled?

"You already knew, didn't you, dude?" Cosme asks. I un-derstand that he's really worried about me.

I also understand that my revelation has come. ∎

Euthanasia

ERIKA MERGRUEN

ROOM 657. FIRST FLOOR

When I'm by your side, I watch your eyelids. Sometimes I press on them, lovingly, with the index finger of my right hand. I hope you'll open your eyes, surprised, so I can see how your pupils dilate as you listen to the purr of the machines that surround you. And I'll be happy, and I'll tell you that story about the cat that appears and disappears in an imaginary land.

When I'm far away, your eyelids go with me. I discover them in your teddy bear's ears, in crusts of bread and in the figures trapped in the mosaic tile around the shower. Then my throat is blocked by the certainty that they will never open. If I'm at home, I go out; if I'm out, I go in. I search—in the trees, in a red stoplight, in a car's windshield, in the cups on the dish rack and in the mirror in the hallway—for the smiling cat that can show me the way out.

When I'm by your side, I watch your eyelids while I imagine your voice: your cries when I said you couldn't have candy for a snack, your bursts of laughter when the circus clowns bonked each other with big sponge bats, your nervous whispers as you described the monster that lurked under your bed. But, as the days go by, your voice belongs more and more to the imaginary land. In this room I can only hear the stupid purring of the machines.

I open your eyelids with my thumbs. I search in your eyeballs for the path that will lead you back. I call you by your name, Daniel, and I wait in vain for your fingers to tighten around my hand.

Your little limp body, doesn't respond. Your eyes turn back until they are all white. The machines go quiet. Now the purring comes from the smiling cat curled up on the crisp pillow of your hospital bed.

ROOM 576. SECOND FLOOR

When I'm by your side, I watch your eyelids. Sometimes I press on them, softly, with the index finger of my right hand. I hope you'll open your eyes, surprised, so I can see how your pupils dilate as you listen to the purr of the machines that surround you. And I'll calm you down, and I'll tell you that story of the cat that appears and disappears in an imaginary land.

When I'm far away, your eyelids follow me. I discover them in your balls of wool, in the beads on your rosary and in the figures trapped in the mosaic tile around the shower. Then my throat is blocked by the uncertainty that they will someday open. If I'm at home, I go out; if I'm out, I go in.

I search—in the trees, in a red stoplight, in a car's wind-shield, in the cups on the dish rack and in the mirror in the hallway—for the smiling cat that can show me the way out.

When I'm by your side, I watch your eyelids while I imagine your voice: your yelling when someone spilled dark liquid on the white carpet, your bursts of laughter when the kids didn't quite manage to reach the *piñata*, your whispers when the priest lifted the Host above the altar. But, as the days go by, your voice belongs more and more to the imaginary land. In this room I can only hear the monotonous purring of the machines.

I open your eyelids with my thumbs. I search in your eyeballs for the path that will let you find peace. I call you by your name, Margarita, and I wait in vain for your fingers to tighten around my hand.

Your withered limp body, doesn't respond. Your eyes turn back until they are all white. The machines go quiet. Now the purring comes from the smiling cat curled up on the crisp pillow of your hospital bed.

ROOM 756. THIRD FLOOR

When I'm by your side, I watch your eyelids. Sometimes I press on them with the index finger of my left hand. I hope you'll open your eyes, surprised, so I can see how your pupils dilate as you listen to the purr of the machines that surround you. And I'll resign myself, and I' ll remember that story about the cat that appears and disappears in an imaginary land.

When I'm far away, your eyelids pursue me. I discover them in the folds of our bed, in the buttons on your shirts and in the figures trapped in the mosaic tile around the shower. Then my throat is blocked by the certainty that they will someday open. If I'm at home, I go out; if I'm out, I go in. I search—in the trees, in a red stoplight, in a car's windshield, in the cups on the dish rack and in the mirror in the hallway—for the smiling cat that can show me the way out.

When I'm by your side, I watch your eyelids while I imagine your voice: your cries when you got home drunk after a night out, your bursts of laughter as you threatened to give the kids a smack on the head, your whispers when you told me you felt ashamed around your family. But, as the days go by, your voice belongs more and more to the imaginary land. In this room I only hear the gentle purring of the machines.

I open your eyelids with my thumbs. I search in your eyeballs for the path that will never let you return. I call you by your name, Fernando, and I wait in vain for your fingers to tighten around my hand.

Your hardy limp body, doesn't respond. Your eyes turn back until they are all white. The machines go quiet. Now the purring comes from the smiling cat curled up on the crisp pillow of your hospital bed.

MORGUE. BASEMENT

FIRST FLOOR: Álvarez, Daniel. Sex: male. Age: 5 years 3 months. Cause of death: multiple trauma due to traffic accident. The deceased was in a comatose state for three months.

SECOND FLOOR: Mújica, Margarita. Sex: female. Age: 81 years 10 months. Cause of death: pulmonary metastases. The deceased contracted cancer of the colon one year earlier.

THIRD FLOOR: De los Monteros, Fernando. Sex: male. Age: 39 years 1 month. Cause of death: hyperosmolar nonketotic coma due to diabetes. The deceased was diagnosed with diabetes mellitus 3 years earlier. ∎

Rottweiler

ISAÍ MORENO

The people of Transval Street often wondered why Octavito couldn't hear on his left side. "Come here, Octavito," they'd say, and he could only hear them if they happened to be on his good side. They had no idea that he had also been mute for three days, including the three troubled nights he spent tossing and turning under the covers in an unending nightmare until his parents dragged him out of it. In fact, not many people spoke of the matter, which freed Octavito and his older sister Ani from inventing explanations.

Those were days of extreme heat, heat that discolors the green leaves of bushes and trees with no mercy, weakens the soul, kills us slowly while the planet crosses Canis Major: the dog days that do no one any good. Everybody knows it from the drowsiness that hangs over the *colonia*, that poisons Transval, all of Romero Rubio, crossing Oceanía and winding its way through the streets around the Peñón, near where Octavito's twin brother was buried.

Ani, Octavito, and their parents often took walks around the Glorieta Africa, the round plaza in the middle of their neighborhood. There the streets met—Jericó and Asia and Africa formed an isosceles triangle with the plaza at its apex. In the plaza, a park. In the middle, a little library. And the slides, the dilapidated seesaw that hardly any children used anymore. It was different before: when they were younger, Octavito and his sister would roller-skate there, until Ani broke her leg. Then they would go to take Chiquis for his walks. As soon as his chain came off, he would shake his white hair—like cotton, when it was clean—and start running in circles just like the cars driving around the plaza. Back then only good people would come to the park, with little children on the jungle gym, balloons that sometimes slipped out of their still-clumsy hands, brightening up the circle of sky above the plaza with their colors. Then the two figures appeared from the Peñón, one tall and fit, the other smaller and stouter. Their skin was very dark.

No one knew them. They also thought Africa Park was a nice place to walk their dogs.

Some say that dogs and their owners look alike, and the pair who claimed the plaza as their territory could have served as evidence for the claim—the Rottweilers at the ends of their chains were tough and muscular, with flat noses and huge heads. Octavito and Ani didn't tell their parents that Africa Park was growing ever more empty or that it looked sad in the afternoon. The two new guys stood watching from one side of the park. At the other, Ani and Octavito with Chiquis. What a standoff! When the invaders arrived, the local parents did what they usually do: they began to gather up their children and their dogs. The Rottweilers barked as if issuing a challenge. This time the kids kept coming, perhaps out of inertia or because the heat kept them from thinking straight. They kept coming. And who would tell them not to? The two men's dark dogs urinated all over the park. Who could expect Chiquis, little as he was, to understand matters of territory? Only Octavito wrinkled his forehead when he saw the dogs slobbering on the other side, with their reddened eyes locked on Chiquis. That wouldn't do, frowning at the strangers.

Octavito remembered the day when his grandmother— may she rest in peace— took him along to buy groceries and gas for the stove. The streets were deserted. The men from the Peñón are coming, people said. Get back to your houses. Don't go out. But his grandmother needed gas. Octavito walked by her side as they made their way home. The gangs from all around were on the corner. In their hands were stones, sticks, chains.

But they paused for a moment. Go on through, *señora*. They looked on respectfully. And Octavito's grandmother told him nothing bad would happen. Come along, sweetie. Nowadays there is no respect for old people and children. A couple of times Octavito passed by the plaza on the way to the market, holding hands with his mother, and he didn't mention the strangers. On the way back, going down Damasco Street to get to Transval, they would buy *pan dulce* fresh out of the oven from Aunt Elia's bakery. Eating it with milk was one of the greatest pleasures of the *colonia* Romero Rubio. Many people came from other neighborhoods to buy the flaky pastry, or settled for sampling the pieces displayed on trays in the shop: never too sweet, its taste stayed on your tongue until the next day.

Ani was the only person Octavito told when the Rottweilers began to appear in his dreams. They chased after him at night, their jaws dripping. Ani told him it was just his imagination. They couldn't stop going to the park just for that. Just think, not taking Chiquis for his walks... Where else could they take him? To the other side of Oceanía, where everything was dirty and dangerous? Don't be a scaredy-cat, Octavio. Ani talked like that because girls like her, who sometimes dress like young women and start to draw glances from the neighborhood boys, are not afraid of anything. After breaking her leg and keeping it in a cast for three months, she put on her skates once again. Octavito didn't skate anymore. She got back to it in the plaza until her father gave her a stern talking-to. A young lady willing to break her other leg, or the same one again, doesn't foul up her life with pessimistic thinking. The newcomers occupied their side of the park and she and her brother kept to their own, in silence. On one side, Chiquis. On the other, the Rottweilers.

So Octavito stayed quiet. He kept his nightmares to himself: one of the Rottweilers reached for him as he clung to the edge of the bed, as far away as his frantic escape could take him. Sometimes the animal climbed up his body while he slept. The image of the dog remains in his dreams. It sniffs every inch of his face. It pores over him. Its breath stinks. The creature's weight crushes his chest, he can't breathe, until he wakes up sweating and smothers his scream so they won't call him a scaredy-cat or say he's paranoid. He even forgot what he was learning in school.

Two days before the incident that filled the *colonia* with strangeness and clamor, when police patrols became normal in the area, Octavito thought he noticed one of the newcomers looking with interest at Ani. Or maybe at Chiquis, whose chain was in his sister's hand. In any case, it was not a friendly glance. What's more, he was sure that the man, now more brazen in the park, bolder and ruder, loosened the Rottweiler's chain as he looked at her. He seemed to be whispering something to his companion, who also looked in their direction. It was certain, they were talking about them. Dogs like Chiquis are restless and persistent. They don't shy away from any animal of any size and they have no sense of danger, so the little animal growled at the murderous dogs. Ani tried to calm him down. What's gotten into you today, Chiquis? Settle down, boy. In those days, no one came to the park in the afternoon. Patrols went by. Octavito had decided he didn't want them to take Chiquis to the park anymore. He'd had enough. The next day, unceasing rain kept them from going out to face his fears. They focused on their homework. He on the horror of fractions. She on spelling.

On the unmentionable day, suffering from a lack of words in his mouth as they headed down Damasco Street toward the plaza, Octavito avoided begging Ani to forget about their walk. He thought it would be better for her to witness the threatening, suspicious, filthy stare of the larger man to convince her that it would be better not to come back, at least for a while. Then there would be time for someone to report the unbearable situation to the police. They kept on walking. They crossed the plaza carefully, watching out for indifferent cars driven by drained people with bags under their eyes, blinded by the sunlight. Octavito looked around for the criminals. In front of them he saw nothing. There was nothing to his right, either, but there was something on the side of his healthy ear, and it was closer to them than he'd thought. Maybe the men had crossed Africa Street just as Octavito and his sister came up Damasco. Or maybe as they were leaving. The taller one smiled. The Rottweiler's loose chain in his hand. And Chiquis growled recklessly. Octavito would have liked to tie his snout shut with his scarf. Please don't bark, he begged. He kept on growling. The other man was amused, watching how his monster pulled at the chain. His companion laughed when they looked at each other.

And Ani? Holding tight to Chiquis' chain. Not afraid but alert. A Rottweiler's bark was no worse than a broken leg. Nor was an obscene laugh, as bad as that seemed. Octavito was the only one to foresee the inevitable. The man releasing a Rottweiler's chain, its huge head and its eyes shot through with bright red, coming for his Chiquis like a wild predator. A chill ran through his legs and up his thighs, there was a hole in his stomach. He could still hear fine on his left side. The animal was already loose, Chiquis tugging at his leash, unconscious of what it all meant. Horror. Horrible. The Dog Star above. Then Ani, protective, not paralyzed like her brother, crouched down, took their little dog in her arms and held him close. Shhh, she whispered, everything's alright, Chiquis. The Rottweiler paused. Octavito had time to admire what his sister had done. She was so clever, but at the same time he was struck by the certainty that the animal would leap on her instead, or on both of them, both together, before he heard from his left ear for the last time. First the dull explosion, like a firecracker, then two more. Very loud. Who knows who was shooting at the two men—they tried and failed to run away. The Rottweilers fled from the sound of the shots. Chiquis... poor Chiquis, Ani felt him trembling in her arms, as if he too had taken a sudden bullet. He whined. She didn't let go of him, or of Octavito, who held his hand up to his ear and took it away with blood on his palm.

The echoes of the gunshots reached Transval. There was a shiver down Oceanía Street, all the way to the edges of the Peñón and the West.

Three days. Octavito had gone three days without a voice to explain to everyone who asked what had happened.

People in blue uniforms. People with recording devices in their hands. Who was shooting? Do you know why? You were the closest witness to the events, son. He wouldn't have answered anyway, because they asked him from the side of his deaf ear. To the right he heard Chiquis breathing, asleep on the rug. ■

The Others

YURI HERRERA

On my way home from work for the first time I saw the terrible man: with three paws on the ground and the fourth clutching a tool. I was unable to make out his features: a cascade of beard and matted hair that protruded from the bottom of his neck obscured his face and at the same time the task at which he labored. I passed him again at lunchtime; the sun continued in free fall, but the man persisted without noticing the delta of pedestrians around him. I managed to catch a glimpse of him from the front: he was sweating.

On one side of the plaza was the office where I had to go mid-afternoon. Clara was already there, wringing her hands and smiling a small, quivering smile. She had become nervous at the last minute. All this time she'd been calm, since deciding ominously to take the test herself the day she accompanied a friend, until reaching the doors of the place and asking herself: *and what if?* What if she had something to worry about? What if the test was positive? What if this was her time?

She was my first girlfriend. The first I had sex with at least. It never occurred to me that something bad might happen, and so I assumed the role of a man of the world, solid, unflappable, experienced, cocky, and told her:

"Don't worry, kitten, look, we'll think really hard, and you'll see there's nothing to worry about."

She looked at me confused. What was I talking about.

"Remember the person you were with," or "people," I added as a mere formality, generous. "Try to think if there's anything that freaks you out, surely not."

She looked at me again surprised, blinking, and then, without moving her eyes, looked inward. I turned toward the plaza while Clara contemplated her past. The terrible man applied his tool with dull blows against a log. I was able to see that he had several more logs, long and thick like an arm, and that his tool was little more than an ax, a kind of sharpened stone.

"Let's see," Clara said... "Perhaps... No, it's best if I start from the beginning."

"She took a pen out of her purse and unfolded a newspaper on the bench where we were sitting. She looked tense, Clara; I caressed her cheek and said Calm down, kitten.

"Okay, first, obviously..." she said, and wrote some initials in the newspaper's margin. *ECJ*.

Her first boyfriend. I don't know why, but it seemed tender.

She hesitated, then wrote *MAH* under them, marked through them, wrote *LCH* and said yes. She thought for a few seconds, the tip of the pen between her teeth, and then wrote down, all at once:

ABS

NCC

DFT

RCV

JMP

She wrote *UMM* beside the third and fourth and drew a very elegant bracket to indicate that those initials went there, that it was important that they were like that. Like this: *UMM!}*

Later she seemed to forget why I was with her; in reality she seemed to forget completely the objective of the memory exercise because the light returned to her face and she began to have fun. She said:

"The guy from the party at Imanol, the bald guy, what was his name?... oh, yeah," and she wrote initials in a strange, vague way: *KW,* or that delicately seemed to coincide with those of an acquaintance of mine: *LRB.*

And also:

"The one from the reggae festival, his last name was... yes, but his name...?" and she wrote down" *D?R.*

A couple of times she wrote a single letter with an annotation to the side, for example: *A (Sandra's friend).*

When she arrived to the 23rd initial she remembered that I was there, she raised her pen, and said:

"Oh, I'm sorry… I shouldn't…" she closed the paper and put it away, "besides I don't know anything, it's best we just wait."

So we did, in silence. I wanted to say something but I didn't know anything to say that that wouldn't sound pathetic. Besides, all of a sudden, I was overcome by a feeling of fragility that I was afraid would destroy me. And this image: my body like a bomb, my veins a conduit of an accursed fluid, me something that she had to run away from. Pins, needles, spikes causing me to explode. My hand began to tremble and I put it in my pants pocket.

"It's time for my appointment," Clara said.

I replied, "Let's go," at least I tried, we went into the office, I accompanied her to the examining room where they were waiting for her, she entered, I sat in the waiting room; however, staying there became unbearable, with all the other human bombs, with all those little boys and little girls chewing their fingernails. I fled to the plaza.

The terrible man was on his knees but his body was straight. He had carved deep angular shapes into the logs and had shaped them into something that was a trio of crosses or an arsenal of stakes. He grabbed his object and hit it forcefully against the ground until the logs fit together. He panted and bellowed as he struck it. The pedestrians passed by without paying attention to him. Finally he stopped exerting himself and rested his forehead on the object. He stood up, stumbled, and scanned his surroundings. I could see him: his eyes were almost transparent, and he had a continental stain on his right cheek. He fixed his stare on a point where nothing was happening and turned toward it. Before I reached the edge of the plaza a car stopped exactly in that spot. A man in a tailored suit and dark glasses got out and the terrible man walked up to him as if to hand him something, but instead he raised his terrible object and let it fall on the man's neck.

"Are you still alive?" someone asked from behind.

Clara. Clara with a huge and fleshy smile.

"Of course there was nothing to worry about, silly," she said, and it hit me. "What's going on over there?"

A small crowd gathered around the spot where the man and the subject were. I couldn't make anything out, but I was able to see, above the bystanders' heads, the terrible man's bloodied object raised, its points glistening red. ◼

Originally published in El Perro (literary magazine)

Questions about the Spread of Mildew

ÚRSULA FUENTESBERAIN

I examine the water spots on the ceiling. They are black. They are swirly like traces of smoke.

While I lie in our bed, looking at the ceiling, I can trace the silhouette of a baby that reminds me of Daher. My son is not in his crib. Did you take him to daycare? And Omar, why did you leave for the bank so early? You didn't want to bother me? What if I told you about all the things I do instead of writing my thesis while I wait for you and Daher to come home?

I alphabetize our records: Arrolladora Banda El Limón, Banda Machos, B.B. King, Cole Porter, El Recodo, Elvis Presley, Frank Sinatra.

Do you remember that when we had been dating for about a month, I made you a mixtape with my favorite songs? You wanted to know why I only listened to gringo music for old people. I told you that when I was twelve years old I spent a summer in Tucson hanging out in the kitchen of the diner where my grandma used to work while my mother went to pick limes and tangerines in northern Arizona. There, while sitting on the pistachio green booths, I heard "Unforgettable," "Fly Me to the Moon" and "Always on my Mind" for the first time. My Granny gave me a quarter every day so I could play the individual jukeboxes in each one of the booths, and I pulled out my English/Spanish dictionary so I could select the three songs with words unknown to me.

When Daher was restless, I'd place the earphones to my belly and play him "The Tennessee Waltz", "Blueberry Hill", "What Difference a Day Makes" or some other slow song by Tony Bennett. You'd get jealous because you wanted to play him one of your records, but *banda* music and *cumbia* cannot lull a baby. You confessed that you were afraid that he'd be labeled a faggot if he was ever heard singing old people's music in English. I used to tell you that it would be ok if our son had tastes that were different from the people in Hermosillo, plus we had named him Daher: like the highest peak of a mountain, the one that stands out.

I keep arranging my records: Intocable, Joan Sebastian, Johnny Cash, La Sonora Santanera, Nina Simone.

Now, when you are not here, time is different.

I sense sounds that I'd never heard in the building before: spoons that stir the sugar in the coffee cups, the flapping sound of the clothes hanging on the roof clothesline, hands peeling vegetables, fingers drumming on a countertop, a little babbling mouth, the refrigerator sighing, a family of bats unfolding their wings and flying out into the twilight from our window sill.

The first time I saw bats, I asked you to kill them. I told you that those winged mice made me sick. You took me back to the window and showed me how they hunted insects. People from my town say that bats are guardians, they not only eat bugs but souls, that is why you have to respect them, you told me, and you made room between your chest and arm so I could cuddle with you close to the window. Their bodies flew in eights and z's and other unidentified signs by the purple clouds. When the sun fell down we could no longer see them. You opened the window and told me to hear closely. I knew that bats send out ultrasound waves and use some kind of sonar to navigate and find their prey in the dark, but I would never had imagined what I heard when I pull my head out of the window, their clicking sounds were like invisible paths.

I take a bath. I turn on just the hot water. I like to look in the mirror and find the steam.

I masturbate furiously. I can't ever cum.

I listen to that record in which Nat King Cole sings in Spanish. My Granny was playing it the first time you came to my house to watch TV. You tried to kiss me, but I dodged you. I asked you to hold me a little. I had to imprint that moment in my brain and I rested my head on your shoulder. It was me who kissed you afterwards. Do you know the forces brought into action when two mouths come in contact?

When a person dies, body heat drops one degree Celsius per hour until it reaches room temperature. Then the decomposition begins. But what happens to a body that's on fire? How long does it take a tiny body of only twelve kilos to disintegrate in a room that's seven hundred degrees Celsius? And what about forty nine bodies that are just as small?

You hate it when I ask you questions that you don't know how to answer, but I've been like that since I was a kid. When I was eight years old, I pestered my Granny, until she bought me The World's Almanac and Book of Facts. From it I learned why Jews marked their homes with lamb's blood, what makes up carbon monoxide, who Herod was and how long it takes a person to faint when experiencing extreme pain.

Estás perdiendo el tiempo...pensando, pensando, Nat sings. His tongue rolls over the r's in slow motion like a wave of lava.

I climb on the bookcase, on the TV stand, onto the shelves with the toys. If we drew an algorithm to calculate the entropy of reaction over our ceiling, do you think the traces would look like the residual coffee grounds that revealed to you that I was expecting Daher? How would the fire spread if the curtains caught on fire? What could have been the longitude of the first flames that burned through the daycare center's awning?

While I'm perched over the cupboard, I examine the mold spots on the kitchen ceiling. Could there be a mathematical formula to predict the spread of mildew?

I put on that green dress that you like so much. I take it off and put it on again, just so I can feel it against my skin. I can barely perceive its satiny caress. I miss your hands.

I brew some coffee; not to drink it, but to watch its vapor in the dark. My college books explain how Joule was able to determine the mechanical equivalent of 4,180 calories. Plastromancy is nowhere to be found in my books, but it does show up in Google, and there it says that if you throw a turtle's shell in the fire and it shows pointed patterns, a loved one will leave you.

My professors say that a chemist only considers an answer valid if it can be proven in a lab, but I think that the origins of an explanation are irrelevant.

I look for my pills. I search through my drawers, I empty the closets, I check under the furniture and between the books. Damn you, Omar! Did you flush them down the toilet again?

I break all of our china. It pisses me off when you don't understand that the pills help me so I won't need to find answers.

I see the terrified look on your face when you come through the door. I throw myself at your feet. I say to you, Omar, where is my baby? Is he at the hospital now? Why was he one of the last children who were pulled out of the daycare? Did they took him out from the opening that one of the parents made with his pick-up truck? What if we were wrong? Are you sure that was his body? What if under the headstone labelled Daher Omar Valenzuela Contreras lies a child that is not our son?

You pick up the broken plates without looking at me. Once the floor is clean, you pack your things.

I watch you sleep in Daher's room, in the bed we bought him for when he grows out of the crib. Why don't you ever sleep in our bed? Do you see my body drowning in a sea of vomit and white pills?

You tried to wake me up. You shook me, cleaned up the vomit, blew into my mouth, and gave me chest compressions. When did you realize that I was no longer there?

I unpack your bags. I carefully put every tie back in its place in our closet, and place every shirt on its hanger. Did you know that two isolated systems can remain in thermal equilibrium when they come in contact as long as "contact" means an exchange of heat, but not of particles?

When you wake up and see what I did, you fall to the floor, curl up and then you cry. I hug you, but you shudder and jolt away. Why do you want me here if you are gone? I have no tears left for the dead! you yell at me. You get up and take all your documents out of the desk and leave without looking back.

I scratch at the door that you slam as you leave. I howl your name. I curse you. I sink my teeth into the frames of the doors. I pick up the scissors and cut up the sheets and reduce them to shreds. I tear up the pillows until they are just crumbles of white pillow stuffing.

I play the Nat King Cole record and pull the dress on. When my head surfaces through the green satin, the bed is made and the pillows are intact. My pills are back on my night table where I always keep them.

I need to take a higher dose tonight, so that when you and Daher get home, you can find me calm. I'll prepare Daher a warm bottle of milk, and I'll serve you shredded beef tacos. I'll show you how much progress I've made on my thesis and when I take Daher to his crib, I'll tell him that when he starts kindergarten, his mom won't be a pharmacy employee anymore, but a graduated Chemist.

I take a pill for every hour that I wait. I close my eyes; Nat lulls me to sleep: *Por lo que más tú quieras, ¿hasta cuándo? ¿hasta cuándo?*

I wake up and you're not in bed. Why did you leave for work so early? I see Daher's silhouette on the ceiling. He's not in his crib. Did you take him to daycare? n

This short story was a finalist at the 2°. Premio Nacional de Cuento Fantástico Amparo Dávila

Kilimanjaro

LOREA CANALES

—The least, the very least that the State should guarantee is our safety, and it can't even do that.

Then, she dialed Luis and told him pretty much the same thing, but with him she could appear more vulnerable.

—I don't know what to do. Miguel has told me not to call him because his phones could be tapped, but we landed past eleven this evening, and I don't even know what hotel to stay in.

—Give me a second, I'm making you a reservation right now. Do you think Miguel will notice if I book it with my credit card?

—I dunno, I brought cash too. He also gave me two credit cards. Why don't I just give you the credit card number?

—How long are you going to stay there?

—I dunno, he told me to start looking for apartments. He wants to buy. I don't know. Ever since this thing with Jorge happened, I'm afraid someone might hurt us. I'm scared.

They said goodbye and he promised to pay her a visit. Luis made her reservations at the Waldorf Astoria, and as soon as she walked into the gigantic lobby, which takes up an entire block, Margarita realized that they wouldn't run the risk of being found there. It was such a crowded public place that even at one in the morning anybody could hang around and not raise any suspicions. Isabela was so agitated after the flight that even though she said she was hungry, she fell asleep before their order of chicken fingers were delivered to their room. She wanted to text Miguel to tell him where she was, but he had already told her that *he* would contact her through one of the cell phones he gave her. She felt so disconnected from her husband. Who was Lucia? Why did she send him so many pictures? And what about herself? It's not like she expected Miguel to always remain faithful to her; that was impossible, but now, over the years she really had believed that when he was away from her, he was actually working. At least she had Luis too. Margarita went to sleep comforting herself with the prospect of all that shopping that she would do the next morning, and thinking about her girlfriends who lived there.

Isabela woke up at five in the morning. For more than an hour, Margarita tried to get her to sleep some more. Margarita had spent the whole night awake and had just fallen asleep. She turned on the TV to try to distract Isabela. Fortunately she found a 24—hour cartoon channel, but by that time she couldn't get rest anymore. She had never felt so lonely and vulnerable before, not even when she came to have an abortion.

Back then, she was twenty years old and she had been dating Alex for four years. What started as not so innocent kissing turned into petting that became more daring and more daring. They sat together in broad daylight in Margarita's living room, where her brothers and the maids passed them by with the clear intention of monitoring them. Whistling and clapping, that's how they warned them. They used to spend the whole afternoon in front of the TV, while Alex's hand moved slowly closer, about an inch per hour or even slower. This way, it took him months, years, to arrive to his destination. Margarita had anticipated and desired this. She was also curious about getting it on with him and making him feel the same chills or maybe electricity she felt. She remembered the first time she realized Alex had an erection. They were kissing goodbye, nothing special at all. They were boyfriend and girlfriend, they kissed and had permission to do that much. Anything beyond that was a transgression that lead to sin and emptied into an irreversible cesspool: the loss of her virginity. That's what she had been taught to believe. That was the point at which you fell into the abyss of evil, which led straight to eternal damnation. Margarita was still a long way from losing her virginity, three years to be exact. She saw something growing in Alex's pants and became scared. She stopped kissing him, backed away and pointed at the bulge with her eyes. Alex laughed unashamedly as if this were something that happened to him often.

—Oh! —he said smiling.—That's because I'm wearing boxers today.

It had been a goodbye kiss. The only thing they were allowed. After they finished, Alex headed to his car. His erection was still noticeable. Margarita was frightened. What had just happened? It was just a kiss. She couldn't possibly have such an effect on him. Alex must've been a pervert, a degenerate. She knew those words, but she didn't know what they meant. But, her mind was using them now. There was something abnormal about her boyfriend. She didn't buy the story about the boxers. Ever since she was a child, she had seen her brothers' underwear, washed and folded, in the laundry basket, and she had noticed how they transitioned into the more colorful and fancy boxers that took up at least half of their drawer space. She went upstairs to her room, lay down on her bed and started to cry. She wanted to call him and ask again about what had just happened: if she couldn't trust *him*, then who could she trust? She didn't dare to call any of her friends from school. The dynamics of her group of friends consisted of divulging information, and sometimes distorting it. Margarita had learned not to say too much. There were two girlfriends in her clique that she was close to. She had discussed with them the appropriate rules of dating such as when it was proper to go from a simple peck on the lips to French kissing. But then she had questions: What did dry-humping consist of? Where did the back end and the ass begin? Getting so close as to rub yourself against his body, which was quite enjoyable by the way, would that constitute some sort of violation? The night they had discussed the rules of kissing, her two best friends had boyfriends, but now one of them had broken up, and the other one didn't seem to get along that well with hers. Margarita didn't feel like making comparisons or talking to them them. She didn't want to feel watched or judged. But she had to talk to someone. She reached for a basket where she kept fashion magazines, and threw some on the bed where she could see them. With her other hand, she dried her tears. She was glancing through an old Cosmo when Daniel, her youngest brother, walked into her room. It was unusual for Daniel to come see her. Surely he wanted something from her. Margarita became defensive.

—I won't lend you my car —she said before he could even open his mouth. Daniel had crashed his a week before, and most likely the car was still at the body shop.

—How did you know that I wanted to borrow your car? —Daniel asked as he jumped onto the bed next to her. Though he was closest to her in age, only two years older, she had argued more with him than with anyone else. He was stronger, but Margarita was meaner. That was established the day she smashed his fingers on purpose by slamming the fridge door on his hand. Eventually they stopped fighting so much, to the point that they could go to the same parties and even had friends in common.

—Do you know Clara Sanchez?

Margarita searched her memory. The name didn't ring a bell. She shook her head without taking her eyes off her magazine. She was wondering if she could ask her brother such a question.

—Why are you asking?

—I wanted to ask her out. Isn't she in your class?

—Nope, doesn't ring a bell. What does she look like?

—Short. Blond. Her hair is this long.

—Oh, I know now: Big boobs? Cute?

—That's the one!

—She's a senior. How did you meet her?

—At the party last week.

—You mean at Renata Cassassus' party.

—Yeah, why didn't you go? It was at a real dope country house by Cuajimalpa. They had a mini rodeo.

—I don't remember what Alex had going on that day. I think we went to his grandma's house. So how was it? Did you get drunk?

—Just a little, nothing serious.

—Did you kiss her?

—Stop it! Why so many questions?

—You kissed her! What a slut! That's why you want to ask her out. Did you have a boner?

—What's with you?!

Daniel grabbed one of her pillows and hit her across the face with it. She turned to him and suddenly, in a serious but warm tone, she asked again:

—No, bro, really. I want to know if you get a boner just from kissing.

—It depends.

—On what?

—The kiss...

—Does it depend on the boxers?

—What?!

Margarita didn't want to give further explanations. She was convinced Alex was lying, but Daniel seemed intrigued by her question.

—No, it doesn't depend on the boxers at all.

Margarita raised her eyebrows as if saying: I knew it. But Daniel went on:

—Getting or not getting a boner depends on the kiss. But whether it's visible or not, that has to do with the under-wear or the pants you're wearing. If you're wearing jeans and briefs, it's almost impossible to see. Meaning, you get hard, but it stays stuffed in your pants. But if you're at the beach wearing boxers and linen pants, then... whooops!.

He made a hand gesture pointing up and imitating the type of erection Margarita had just witnessed.

—Then, it's like jelly.

—How so?

—It all depends on the mold.

—I'd rather not think about my tweety like that, but if you want to think about it that way.

—Tweety! That's what you call it?

—Yep —said Daniel, suddenly embarrassed to be having this conversation with his sister.

—Does every guy give it a name? —Margarita asked. She wouldn't want to let this intimate opportunity pass.

—I don't know if every guy...

Margarita felt better. Alex wasn't lying. He was no pervert. She realized that she had no clue about the male world. Guys name their penises! She was eager to learn more.

—Do you want me to get you Clara's number? Or did that slut already give it to you?

Margarita grabbed her pillow and hit her brother back. This was the very first time they trusted each other, Margarita thought as she watched her daughter who was still distracted by the TV and regretted not being able to sleep more. Four years after this revealing conversation with her brother, she thought she knew Alex perfectly well. She knew that his dick was called Margarito, in her honor. She knew that he liked to be touched softly, that he had to cum while he was with her or afterwards, otherwise he would suffer horrible cramps in his balls, called *blue balls*. She loved it when he touched her. Week after week, year after year, as hiking enthusiasts they had climbed the seven peaks. Only the Everest remained. He had already sucked her nipples (Mount Carstensz, 16,023 feet high), she really loved it once she overcame her shame. He had touched her with his fingers (Vinson Massif, 16,050 feet). He fingered her (Mount Elbrus, 18,510 feet). She gave him a handjob,

(Mount Kilimanjaro, 19,341 feet). He went down on her (Mount Logan, 19,551 feet). Lastly, she had given him a blowjob, (Aconcagua, 22,837 feet). She didn't enjoy it very much, but she didn't feel disgusted either. Regina had confessed to her that she threw up.

—That's too bad, Margarito.

That's what she used to say every time —which happened a lot—, that he couldn't cum. She never dared to ask what he did with his wet pants afterwards, but judging from her brothers' attitude, she was sure that he just threw them into the hamper with the rest of the dirty clothes without even bothering to think that somebody else had to wash them. She even thought about asking the maid if they had ever noticed anything before, but she didn't even know how to bring up the topic. She simply didn't want to have that type of relationship with the help, or the level of complicity that would inevitably result from it.

It took her more or less a year to prepare to climb Mount Everest. They needed a weekend alone, by themselves, without family and friends suspecting anything. They had to make sure that the help wouldn't snitch. Margarita asked if she should take birth control pills, but Alex said it wasn't necessary. He would wear a condom. Alex was not a virgin. At fourteen, his uncle took him to a brothel. He admitted that he didn't enjoy the experience or the one-night stands he had with some foreign girls in Acapulco. He was convinced that with Margarita it would be different. Finally, the day arrived. Fifteen of Margarita's friends were heading to a ranch in Veracruz. She asked her parents for permission to go and assured her friends that she'd go, but she canceled at the last minute by pretending to be sick. He found a way to use a friend's house in Las Brisas. Since his friend's family didn't know them, the maids and other help wouldn't be a problem. And since it was a house, no one would see them going in or coming out. They would drive to Acapulco. Before the trip, Margarita had second thoughts and she called him. Shouldn't we wait until marriage? Wouldn't it be better to do it during their honeymoon? Alex soothed her. They had nothing to lose. He had two more years before graduation, and he couldn't wait that long. As soon as he graduated, even a year prior, he'd propose. He'd marry her. But this was a different matter. It was exciting, and this adventure would bring them even closer. They had been dating for about four years, and he couldn't wait another week. That's what he said over the phone. Then he stopped talking, and Margarita sensed a warning in his silence. It hurt. Not as much as people said. But it did hurt. She bled. Not much, just a couple of drops. She had brought an extra sheet she bought in Liverpool. She didn't want to stain the ones from the house, though it was barely noticeable. She didn't get to feel the butterflies nor the sparks she used to have when she was with him. She was deeply disappointed. Was that it? Was that all? Alex claimed that this feeling would pass, that little by little it would get better, and that they just needed practice. He even suggested that they watch some porn videos together for learning purposes. Margarita was willing. She wanted to learn. She wanted to satisfy him and to drive him crazy. She gave it her best efforts. The following months, they found the most unsuspected places to get it on: the car, a random corner, the restroom in a restaurant. They took advantage of every single minute of privacy they had. The fifth month, she realized she was pregnant. Ever since she was sexually active, she documented her period on a calendar with the utmost precision. She would anticipate its arrival, and every minute of delay made her anxious. She would wait a day, two, and then the third day she'd start bleeding, confirming that everything was in its place, in its period literally. But the fifth month was November. One day went by and then three days passed. Margarita grew more weary with each hour. She suffered in silence. Alex had no idea, but she did remember that they weren't using condoms every time. He didn't wear one every time. If I pull out before coming, nothing will happen, he assured her. Margarita trusted him. It wasn't possible to get pregnant if he didn't come inside her. Or was it? One week late. Margarita went to the pharmacy and bought two pregnancy tests. That same afternoon, she bought two more. The faint pink line wasn't convincing, but it didn't fade away either. She didn't remember having cried. She didn't remember those moments. Did she picture herself walking down the aisle pregnant? Did she figure the embarrassment of having to tell her parents? She had eaten the cake. She recalled taking a couple of days before telling Alex. When she gave him the news, the pink line in the test was unmistakable.

—I'm not ready for this.

That was his response, with his eyes fixed on his tacos al pastor that he was pretending to eat.—I can't do this.

—What do you want me to do? —she asked quietly.

—I don't know. I don't know. I just can't —Alex pushed his chair back and stood up.

—I have to go.

He left her at the restaurant, without a ride or money for the bill. Most likely he didn't realize it, Margarita figured. He was in total shock. After waiting several minutes for him to return, Margarita called a friend who lived nearby and told her that they had just gotten into a fight. She sensed in her friend's curiosity and pity that she enjoyed the fact that she had fought with Alex. She imagined the malicious gossip and everything they'd say behind her back. She had played her Virginity card and had lost it all. She listened silently as if nothing had happened as her friend talked to her. Then she believed that she had prayed in that moment of total despair, but she wasn't sure. What did happen was that her friend told her about a New York shopping trip that she was planning. Pilar's mother had an apartment there and she was inviting them all. They just needed their airline tickets. Some of them already had tickets to Broadway. Her friend was encouraging her to come.

—Yes, Margarita said.—That sounds cool.

In a matter of seconds, everything was resolved. That same night, she was given permission and money to go shopping. Then she spent hours on her laptop browsing and researching, until she found out about Planned Parenthood. She had found the place. Since she was legally an adult, it wouldn't be a problem. She even had money left over for shopping afterwards. It hurt a little more than losing her virginity, but not that much. She was less than a month pregnant, so it was a simple procedure. She never regretted it. When she returned to Mexico, she broke up with Alex. It was through a simple phonecall. She just told him: it's over. That really hurt her. She cried over Alex for years. Though they were part of the same group of friends, they managed to avoid each other without a problem. They only ran into each other in three different occasions. They never discussed the subject. Nobody ever found out. None of her male friends from back then asked her out again, but she thought it was because they were so possessive and jealous that they didn't want to go out with someone who had dated another guy for so long. When she started dating Miguel, she felt guilty about not being a virgin. She was afraid he'd reject her. One night, after some heavy petting, she confessed to him:

—I'm not a virgin.

—Me neither —Miguel responded.

And he went back to kissing her. ∎

Authors

Alberto Chimal (Toluca México, 1970) Has published dozens of short story books such as 83 novelas, *Grey* and *Éstos son los días* (this one awarded with the Premio Nacional de Cuento INBA 2002). Author of *Los esclavos*, a novel and the essay book La cámara de las maravillas. His second novel *La*  *Torre y el Jardín* was a finalist on 2013 for the international novel award Premio Internacional de Novela Rómulo Gallegos 2013, one of the most prestigious in spanish language.

Chimal teaches Comparative Literature at Universidad Nacional Autónoma de México and workshops at Universidad Iberoamericana and Universidad del Claustro de Sor Juana. He was a jury for Caza de Letras, an internet online workshop-award organized by UNAM throughout 2007 and 2010. Currently he is member of the Sistema Nacional de Creadores de Arte, Mexican institution that sponsors artist s works form several fields.

Some of his writings have been translated to English, French, Italian, Hungarian and Esperanto. He is considered one of the most talented and original writers of his generation, pioneer of digital writing, he posts in his blog ⊕ www.lashistorias.com.mx

 **Erika Mergruen** (Mexico City, 1967) poet and fiction writer. Has published the poetry books *Marverde* (1998), *El El osario* (2001) and *El sueño de las larvas* (2006); the short story books *Las reglas del juego* (2001) and *La piel dorada y otros animalitos* (2009); An autobiobraphy *La ventana, el recuerdo como relato* (2002); flash fiction book *El último espejo* (2013), the novels *La casa que está en todas partes* (2013) and *Todos los vientos* (2015) She a columnist for the newspaper La Jornada Aguascalientes. 🐦 @mergruen

Isaí Moreno (Mexico City, 1967) Writer. He is the author of the novels: Pisot (Awarded with the Juan Rulfo prize for first novel on 1999) and *Adicción* (2004), works that he wrote while obtaining his Ph.D. in Mathematics at the Universidad Autónoma Metropolitana. *El suicidio de una mariposa* (his  third novel, published by Terracota on late 2012) was finalist for the award Premio Rejadorada de Novela Breve 2008 in Valladolid, Spain. He teaches workshops on writing novels and he is teacher-researcher at the Universidad Autónoma de la Ciudad de México in Creative Literature. He collaborates in several literary magazines, cultural supplements and blogs such as Nexos, Letras Libres, La Tempestad, Lado B, Nagari Magazine and others. His short stories have been published in anthologies such as: *Así se acaba el mundo* (Ediciones SM, 2012), *Tierras insólitas* (Almadía, 2013) y *Sólo cuento* (UNAM, 2015). In 2010 he obtained his B.A. in Hispanic Language and Literature with his thesis: *Hacia una estética de la destrucción en la literature.* Since 2012 he is a member of Sistema Nacional de Creadores de Arte de México. 🐦 @isaimoreno.

 **Yuri Herrera** (Actopan, México, 1970). Studied the Bachelor in Political Science at UNAM and Masters in Creative Literature at the University of Texas, El Paso. He has a PhD in Language and Hispanic Literature from University of California (Berkeley). Currently he has a teaching post at Tulane University (New Orleans). His short stories, articles, chronicles and essays have been published in newspapers and magazines from USA, Latinamerica and Spain such as: El País, Reforma, La Jornada, El Malpensante, de Letras Libres, War and Peace, also he has been included in several anthologies. He was founder and editor of the literary magazine *el perro*.

His novels are, *Trabajos del reino* (Periférica, 2008), *Señales que precederán al fin del mundo* (Periférica, 2009), y *La transmigración de los cuerpos* (Periférica, 2013).

Úrsula Fuentesberain (Celaya, Guanajuato 1982). Writer and journalist. Her first short story book is *Esa membrana finísima* (Fondo Editorial Tierra Adentro, 2014). Her short stories have been published in nine anthologies, the most recent ones are *Emergencias: Cuentos mexicanos de jóvenes talentos* (Lectorum, 2015), *Pide un deseo* (Tusquets, 2014) y *Lados B* (Nitro Press, 2014). With the support of the Fulbright-García Robles scholarship, she studied the masters of creative writing at Sarah Lawrence College. The short story included in this collection was a finalist at the 20. Premio Nacional de Cuento Fantástico Amparo Dávila and will be part of the anthology of this same award published by Libros Pimienta.

Lorea Canales Author of *Apenas Marta* y *Los Perros*, acclaimed by the Mexican critic as the best novels of 2011 and 2013. Lorea Canales belongs to a new generation of global writers. *Becoming Marta* published by Amazon Crossing in English was honored with the International Latino Fiction Award, and its publication in Polish.

Lawyer, journalist and novelist she earned her Masters in Law at Georgetown University in Washington DC where she worked as a lawyer before joining the newspaper Reforma as a legal correspondant. She taught Law at ITAM. Since 2000 she lives in New York where se contributes to several Mexican publications. Studied Creative Writing at New York University where she earned her Masters degree in 2010.